THE BIRTHDAY TREE

by Paul Fleischman   pictures by Marcia Sewall

HarperTrophy
A Division of HarperCollins*Publishers*

To my Mother and Father

Library of Congress Cataloging-in-Publication Data
Fleischman, Paul.
    The birthday tree.

    SUMMARY: When Jack goes to sea, his parents
watch as the tree planted at his birth reflects
his fortunes and misfortunes.
    [1. Trees—Fiction]   I. Sewall, Marcia.
II. Title.
PZ7.F599233Bi   [E]   78-22155
ISBN 0-06-021915-7
ISBN 0-06-021916-5 lib. bdg.
ISBN 0-06-443246-7 (pbk.)

First Harper Trophy edition, 1991.

Once there was a sailor who fled from the sea. He and his wife had lost three sons to the waves, so they gathered up their belongings in a creaky wheelbarrow and left the water behind them.

"A plague on the sea," said the sailor to his wife. "It whistles a sweet tune to lure the boys out of the hills and down to the boats. But it pipes other tunes as well—shrieking winds and ships splitting on rocks."

At nightfall the sailor cupped his hands to his ears. He could no longer hear the sea.

After another day's walk the sailor took out his spyglass. He could no longer glimpse the sea.

On the third day the sailor and his wife found themselves in a green valley. They could no longer smell the sea.

"It's here we'll put down," said the sailor.

He and his wife built a simple house and planted a farm. They tended chickens and goats and sheep.

Soon they had another son. They named him Jack. To celebrate his birth the sailor planted a tiny apple seedling.

As Jack grew taller, so did the tree. As Jack grew stronger the tree trunk thickened, its limbs fanning out like a peacock's tail.

Jack and the apple tree seemed almost to be one. He swung upside down from its branches. He climbed to the top and looked out over the valley. He lay in its shade during the summer. On rainy days he would sit inside by the window and watch the drops flutter the leaves.

One morning Jack awoke with a chill. His teeth chattered, and his mother covered him with blankets. Still he shivered. Through the window of his room, Jack's mother thought she noticed the leaves of the apple tree shivering as well.

She told her husband what she'd seen.

"Nonsense," he replied.

But that afternoon Jack's father stood gazing at the tree. The air was still, yet the apple leaves trembled on their stems.

"It's so," he muttered.

As the years passed the sailor and his wife noticed that the branches of the tree hung heavy when Jack was sad. When he was happy the limbs stood out straight and proud, and squirrels scampered about the tree.

The sailor and his wife never spoke of the sea. Yet sometimes a strong, salt wind would blow in from the ocean, and the sailor would notice Jack sniffing the air with curiosity. One day the

sailor and his wife looked up
from their work and saw
Jack watching a flock of gulls
squawking high overhead.

"What kind of birds are
those?" asked Jack.

His parents felt afraid, and
said they didn't know.

One summer's morning the sailor and his wife awoke and found Jack's bed empty.

"Jack!" cried his mother.

"Jack, boy!" cried his father. Their voices echoed over the valley. There was no reply.

Then the sailor spotted a meadowlark perched on top of the apple tree. He knew the meadowlark was a bird of the fields. "It's a sign," he said. "Our Jack must be traveling over land."

For three days the meadowlark sat atop the tree. The next morning a white gull was perched in its place. "He's traveling over water now," said the sailor to his wife. "Our Jack has gone to sea."

All summer long the gull stood atop the apple tree. The sailor and his wife were afraid for Jack, and lonely living without him. They wondered where he was and whether he was well, and they watched the tree closely for any news of him.

In the fall the tree was laden with apples and the sailor and his wife made them into cider and pies. The cider was clear and the pies were sweet.

"It's a good sign," said the sailor. "Our Jack is happy."

The nights grew cold. The apple tree lost its leaves to the wind and its bare branches stood out against the winter sky. The sailor inspected the buds and found them closed up tight.

"Jack's snug this winter," he said to his wife.

In spring the buds opened and fresh green leaves crept out. Pink blossoms clustered along the branches and swarms of bees hummed loudly about the tree. Jack's mother ran her fingers through the leaves as though through her son's hair.

"Strong and healthy, our Jack is," she said.

Summer came to the valley, and summer showers. One night a sharp wind sprang up and rain spattered the earth. Suddenly a bolt of lightning stabbed at the tree and lit up every leaf. A limb cracked and crashed to the ground. The sailor and his wife ran to the window.

"Oh Jack!" cried the sailor's wife.

"His ship's been struck!" gasped the sailor.

The tree bucked furiously in the wind and rain. All night the sailor and his wife stayed by the window.

The apple tree survived the storm. But the gull, which had perched atop the tree since Jack had left, was not to be seen.

"Our Jack is traveling no more," said the sailor. "It's shipwrecked, he is—I know it. Stranded on some lonely island."

Then the sailor and his
wife noticed a change
coming over the tree. The
leaves were becoming dry as
paper. "Jack must be thirsty,"
said the sailor's wife, and she
watered the tree.

Only a few apples appeared that fall. The sailor and his wife made them into cider and pies, but the cider was bitter and the pies tasted sour.

Day by day the apple tree sickened. Its limbs bent over like the backs of old men. The squirrels who chased about the branches when Jack was happy no longer came to the tree. The sailor and his wife nursed the tree as if it were Jack himself, but nothing helped.

The nights froze and soon the apple tree dropped its last leaf. Its bare, bony limbs drooped until they scraped the ground. The wind moaned in the branches like a ghost. All day the sailor and his wife sat by the window and stared.

The sailor noticed that the branches hung lower than before. "Jack needs food," he said, and he fertilized the tree.

But the leaves curled and the limbs sagged lower.

"There's no hope," said the sailor to his wife. The apple tree appeared dead.

Winter slowly passed. The sailor and his wife no longer tended the tree. They tried not to look at it.

"Three days' journey is still too close to the sea," said the sailor one day. He and his wife decided to abandon the farm and the apple tree, and move far back into the hills.

"We'll walk till we come to people who've never even heard of the sea," said the sailor.

The next morning the sailor and his wife packed their belongings in their creaky wheelbarrow and headed down the road. They turned for a last look at the apple tree, and behold! The limbs of the tree had picked themselves up off the ground. Tiny green leaves had appeared, and at the top of the tallest branch sat a gull.

"Our Jack is alive," shouted the sailor, "and traveling over the water. He's been rescued!"

Leaves unfurled along the limbs and glowed in the sunlight like stained-glass windows. The blossoms opened and bees thronged about the tree. Squirrels raced along the branches.

For weeks the gull
remained atop the apple tree.
And then one morning the
sailor spotted a meadowlark
in its place.

"Our Jack's left the sea!"
he called to his wife. "He's
traveling over land!"

For three days the meadowlark perched on the tree. The next morning it was gone. In its place was an oriole, busily building its nest on the topmost branch.

"Well," said the sailor to his wife, "Jack's traveling days are over. He's picked himself out a spot and put down."

The sailor and his wife walked back inside the house.

And there was Jack.
Asleep in his old bed.